SURVIVOR DIARIES

AVALANCHE!

SURVIVOR DIARIES

AVALANCHE!

BY TERRY LYNN JOHNSON

HOUGHTON MIFFLIN HARCOURT
Boston   New York

The text was set in Adobe Caslon Pro.
Illustrations by Jani Orban

The Library of Congress has cataloged the paper over board edition as follows:
Names: Johnson, Terry Lynn, author. | Orban, Jani, illustrator.
Title: Avalanche! / by Terry Lynn Johnson ; illustrations by Jani Orban.
Description: Boston ; New York : Houghton Mifflin Harcourt, [2018] | Series: Survivor diaries | Summary: Twelve-year-old twins Ashley and Ryan are tested to the extreme when faced with a powerful avalanche while skiing in Wyoming's Teton Range. Includes survival tips from the National Avalanche Center and U.S. Forest Service.
Identifiers: LCCN 2016057685
Subjects: | CYAC: Survival—Fiction. | Avalanches—Fiction. | Brothers and sisters—Fiction. | Twins—Fiction. | Teton Range (Wyo. and Idaho)—Fiction. | BISAC: JUVENILE FICTION / Action & Adventure / Survival Stories. | JUVENILE FICTION / Nature & the Natural World / Environment. | JUVENILE FICTION / People & Places / United States / General. | JUVENILE FICTION / Sports & Recreation / Winter Sports. | JUVENILE FICTION / Family / Siblings. | JUVENILE FICTION / Animals / Bears.
Classification: LCC PZ7.J63835 Av 2018 | DDC [Fic]—dc23
LC record available at https://lccn.loc.gov/2016057685

ISBN: 978-0-544-97039-7 paper over board
ISBN: 978-1-328-51906-1 paperback

Printed in the United States of America
DOC 10 9 8 7 6 5 4 3 2 1
4500710965

For Mike — an avalanche of creative energy
and charm

CHAPTER ONE

"Tell me how you survived the avalanche," the reporter said. He placed his phone on the kitchen table between us, then pressed Record. With his pen poised over his notepad, he looked at me expectantly. He smelled like grass and ink and summer tomatoes from the garden.

Without thinking, I glanced around for my brother, but he wasn't in sight.

"You sure you don't want to talk to Ryan, too?" Dad asked the reporter, filling his cup with coffee. "He's got a good eye for detail."

"Maybe later." The reporter smiled at me. One tooth along the top was slightly crooked and stuck out. "I want to hear it from Ashley first."

"The avalanche wasn't even the worst part," I began. "But I'll never forget the roar. How fast it all happened. One minute we were skiing, the next we were being swept down the mountain at lightning speed. It just grabbed us and I couldn't stop myself from falling. I couldn't breathe. The snow was everywhere, choking white blizzard in the air. Couldn't see . . ."

"Wait." The reporter stopped recording. "I explained to your parents, Ashley. I'm writing a series about brave kids like you, surviving in the wilderness. Readers will want to know everything you were thinking, everything you did, so they can learn what to do if it happens to them. Where were you, and how did it happen? Try to tell me everything you remember."

He didn't look at Dad, or anyone else. Only me.

I felt suddenly anxious about being part of a series about brave kids. I was used to just being Ashley Hilder, twelve years old, twin sister to the awesome Ryan Hilder. I had never been anything special before, compared to him.

The reporter pressed the red Record button again. "Tell me your story."

I sat back in my chair, trying to conjure up the memory of that day. "It all started with the wolverines."

CHAPTER TWO

Two months earlier

"Try to keep up with your brother, Ash," Dad said.

I had heard that my whole life.

"You have to push yourself if you want to get faster and be the best on the team," he continued.

The *shush*ing from my skis muffled his voice, but I heard what he was saying loud and clear.

Be as good as Ryan. I wanted my dad to be proud of *me,* too.

The guide from the lodge where we were staying had dropped us off at the Chiseler Ditch trailhead. We were here to ski the famous mountains of Wyoming. Snowy peaks rose up like white daggers around us. We had mountains back home in Vermont, but none like these.

The late-March ski conditions were perfect. Fresh snow from yesterday had set us up with pure powder. We'd be making first tracks, which was always my favorite part of alpine touring. The guide told us that the avalanche danger was only moderate below the tree line—a two out of five. It was three out of five, or considerable, in the upper alpine sections, but we were staying low today because of Mom. She wasn't as comfortable on skis as the rest of us.

We stopped for lunch and studied the pamphlet we'd been given at the lodge earlier that morning. It provided information about wolverines along with a map. Some group was doing a study to figure out how recreational activity was affecting the wolverines. They had a sticky trap set on Colt Summit to catch the hairs of passing wolverines.

"Listen to this quote from Douglas Chadwick's *The Wolverine Way*," Ryan said, reading from an excerpt in the pamphlet. "If wolverines have a strategy, it's this: Go hard, and high, and steep, and never back down, not even from the biggest grizzly, and least of all from a mountain." Ryan clawed his hand in front of his face for added drama as he read. "Climb everything: trees, cliffs, avalanche chutes, summits. Eat everybody: alive, dead, long-dead, moose, mouse, fox, frog, its still warm heart or frozen bones. Whatever wolverines do, they do undaunted. They live life as fiercely and relentlessly as it has ever been lived."

"Gross about eating everybody," I said, and tossed a snowball at him.

"Imagine seeing a wolverine for real," Ryan

said, his eyebrows high the way they get when he's excited about a new plan. Ryan always has a new plan.

After lunch, we continued down toward the Marmot Shelter, a heated yurt where Mom said she wanted to take a "proper break." Ryan led, as usual. I was next and then Dad. Mom struggled to keep up behind him. We skied along the trail, which was carved out between snow-swept spruce and fir.

When Ryan sped up, I glanced behind to our parents before racing after him.

"Keep going," Dad called after us. "I'll stay with Mom. We'll meet you at the shelter."

Ryan's backpack, filled with his usual ski touring gear, bounced as he sped along the trail. I knew where he was heading.

"You coming or what?" he said over his shoulder. "We'll have time to check it out if we hurry."

"Wait," I said. "We don't even know where it is."

Ryan stopped and pulled out the map he had stuffed in his pocket after lunch. He pointed to Colt Summit. "Yeah, we do. It's not far. And besides, going off-piste is what you wanted, right?"

I'd always told him I thought skiing was more fun off the established trails. It was what excited me the most about our vacations.

Ryan returned the map to his pocket, then pulled his helmet from his pack and snapped it on over his hat. "I know you want to skin up this face to hit untouched snow." He grinned at me.

I could see Colt Summit now through the trees.

"Eat my dust," Ryan said, pushing off sideways and gaining speed down a slight grade.

"Hey!" I lurched after him.

We sprinted a rowdy race to the next outcrop, but it was no use. I never beat him.

Being twins is hard. Everyone compares you. Even though he's a guy and I'm a girl, we still look alike. Dark hair, dark eyes, pointy chins, and dimples in the same left cheek. We do the same activities. We're even on the same ski team. But people point out right in front of us that he's better at almost everything.

The pack bumped my back as I hit a rough patch, and I stopped to pull my stainless steel water bottle out of the insulated sleeve. The bottle was nearly empty. The frosted Grand Teton, the highest point in the Teton Range and the second highest peak in Wyoming, rose up in the distance, and Colt Summit was just ahead on our right. I blew my breath out in a cloud and wrapped my glove around my ski pole.

When we stopped at the fork in the trail, Ryan took out the map again and pointed at it.

"Look. I was right. Here is where we'd go left to the shelter in Marmot Valley. But the wolverine hair trap is set up there on Colt Summit. Let's go see if we can spot a real wolverine."

Scratching at my hat, I looked behind us. "You sure we have time?"

It had started to snow, adding more powder

9

to our ski. Large flakes melted on my hot face when I gazed up at the peak. I pulled up beside Ryan and reached for one side of the map.

"We'd have to follow the right fork till about here," I said, reading the map we held between us and pointing. "And then cross that ridge before we got to the approach to Colt Summit. We should wait for Mom and Dad."

But after a few minutes of standing still, we got cold. The sweat on our skin began to feel icy. I pulled out my own helmet, put it on, and secured the strap under my chin. We glanced at each other, and then in unison headed up the right fork in the trail, gaining speed to warm up. Ryan led.

"Hurry," he said. "We can be up and back before they catch us if you get moving. But if not, they'll see our tracks and know where we are. No worries, little sister."

Six minutes is apparently very important when it comes to birth order. Ryan never let me forget which one of us was born first.

With enough speed, we headed up a slope and around a tight bend on the edges of our wide touring skis. The air was crisp. When we left the trail, I glanced behind us and smiled at our new tracks in the clean snow. I twisted back to face forward and scanned where I thought our route should take us up to the summit. It was going to be so fun coming down.

The only sounds were our skis *shush*ing in the snow and my ragged breathing in my ears as we pushed upward. Once the terrain got steeper, we stopped to unroll our mohair climbing skins and then attached them to the bottoms of our skis to avoid sliding backwards.

I glided a few strokes, getting used to the feel of not sliding back. My tracks behind me drew straight lines in the snow like two long highway stripes. But when I faced ahead, I spotted different tracks.

"Ry! Look!"

Large oval footprints just like the ones on the pamphlet from the lodge crossed our tracks

and zigzagged ahead. They were almost the size of my boot. "Are we sure they're wolverine? They're so big," I said.

"Wolverines are only, like, thirty-five pounds," Ryan whispered, peering around. "But I read that their paws are as broad as the paws on a hundred-and-twenty-pound wolf. It's so they can walk on top of the snow."

I could clearly see the imprint of the claws. "These must be very fresh," I said, glancing up at the falling snow. "They haven't been covered yet."

The prints bounded ahead toward a crop of conifers shrouded in snow.

"Let's get to that stand of trees over there," Ryan said. "Maybe we'll surprise the wolverine."

The evergreens looked promising, but there was a large open expanse between us and the trees. I waited for Ryan to ski forward first, leaving a good distance between us like we'd learned in avalanche training at our ski club. I remembered if you had to cross avalanche terrain, you shouldn't expose more than one person to danger at a time. I watched him and then followed.

Out in the open, I had a better sense of the sprawling landscape that surrounded us. Mountain ranges spread out in every direction. As our skis broke through the crisp, thin coating of hoarfrost underneath the new layer of snow, we heard a muffled *whump*.

We both froze and looked at each other.

An ominous sliding sound began. I felt the ground move beneath me. With growing horror, I saw the snow around us slab and break away.

"Avalanche!" I screamed.

CHAPTER THREE

Adrenaline surged through me as I realized what was happening. We had skied onto the lip of a dangerously loaded snowfield. It was like a gigantic dinner plate that starts breaking up. I saw cracks and felt the unstable snow shift again beneath me.

"Ash!" I heard Ryan yell, but there was no time.

Our avalanche lessons kicked in to my brain. I pointed my skis to the side and a little down-hill. I had to get past the slab and out of the

path of the sliding avalanche. A churning pile of debris swept around me, broken trees, chunks of ice.

My skis hit something and blew off. I stumbled a moment before I remembered, *swim hard*. I started to do a backstroke toward the trees. Kicking my arms and legs, I tried to stay on the surface of the moving flow. Being in the chaos was nothing like they had told us at the training. How could I swim in this?

Everything seemed to be happening so fast. I spied a tree. When I grabbed hold of its trunk, snow rushed around my head. A big noise, like thunder, boomed behind me. I felt the rumble.

I glanced behind just in time to see the wall of snow begin to envelop me. It ripped me from the tree trunk along with a seething mass of branches. I was swept up and tumbled over and over. No matter which direction I was tossed in, all I could see was empty, cold whiteness. Choking snow everywhere. I was trundled through trees, and felt my right leg twist.

The whole world was collapsing.

I hit something hard and stopped dead. Thickening snow quickly encased me. I only had time to throw one hand in front of my face to make an airway, and the other above my head.

Everything went still.

Darkness.

My panicked breathing roared in my ears. I was dead. I was going to die here unless Ryan escaped the avalanche and came to dig me out. Yes, of course he was okay. He had to be. He was Ryan, the best at everything. And he'd find me and save me. But then I realized we hadn't turned on our avalanche beacons. They were lying at the bottom of the packs. Ryan wouldn't be able to trace my transceiver beneath the snow unless I had it on and was wearing it like we were supposed to.

I needed to conserve my oxygen. Do my counting to slow my breathing. Breathe in four counts. One—two—three—four. Breathe out four counts. One—two—three—four. Once I focused on my breathing, I calmed down, and realized my arm felt cold. It took me another moment to understand why.

It was wind—my arm was above the snow!

I brushed at the top of my helmet. There was less snow than I had imagined. The darkness turned lighter as I clawed at the snow in front of my face. And then suddenly my face was free.

I gulped fresh air.

Frantically, I set to work freeing my other arm. "Ryan!" I screamed. "Where are you? Help!"

There was no response.

I kept digging. With both hands free, I wiggled out of my backpack and scrambled to the surface. I rolled up on top of the snow, blinking my eyes. When I reached up to rub them, I felt my helmet and shakily ripped it off my head.

I stared at the hole I had just been in, and all I could think was, *That was almost my grave.* That lonely hole. Dark and cold. What just happened? Why?

My mind wouldn't focus. I could only sit there, gaping.

I began to shiver. That woke me up. I realized I had to get moving.

"Ryan!" I screamed, but then immediately peered up at the mountain, fearing another slide. I couldn't help screaming again. "Help! Someone! Anyone!"

Desperately, I scanned the area. Nothing but a wide swath of white between the stark trunks of the spruce trees. I'd been swept right off the mountain into a ravine. Tons of snow had slammed into the valley, maybe two hundred feet across. How deep? Where was Ryan?

When I crawled to my feet, a stabbing pain in my knee made me gasp and pitch back down.

And then I saw his ski pole sticking out of the snow.

CHAPTER FOUR

I yanked up my pack, tore it open, and snatched the collapsible shovel from inside. After crawling frantically to the ski pole, I extended the shovel to prepare for digging. I didn't need the avalanche probe to find Ryan. I knew he was buried under the snow near the pole.

My brother was buried under the snow!

I had to move fast. He was going to run out of air. How long since the avalanche? How long did I take after I dug myself out? I had sat for too long in shock. How could I have sat there, wasting precious seconds?

"Hang on, Ry! I'm here, I'm here."

The packed snow was hard to break, even with the shovel. It was fluid at first, but now it had settled like concrete. Carefully digging down along the pole so as not to hit him, I uncovered Ryan's hand. I grabbed it and squeezed.

A cry escaped me when he squeezed back.

So much relief flooded through me, I started to sob. "I've got you."

I began to scrape away more snow with my hands, down to his elbow. It was his right hand, so I knew which way he was facing. Thankfully he had stuck his pole up in time. Otherwise, how would I have known he was down there? *Can't think about that. Keep digging.*

I doubled my speed, desperate to get to his face. Racing the clock. How long?

Was he doing his breathing counts? The blackness and tight, confined space were so fresh in my mind, I knew exactly how he felt down there. Had he filled his lungs before the snow buried him? How much room did he have?

I had to get him. Dig. I worked feverishly. My left glove raked off, my bare hand leaving red smears in the snow. One of the nails on my left hand was broken and bleeding.

I'd dug at least three feet already. How long before I got the snow off his face?

Seconds ticked by. Running out of time. Running out of air. The scene around me was so still. Deathly quiet after all the slamming and crashing and thundering. Snow fell, muffling sounds even more. I was in my own wide-awake nightmare, digging for my brother's life.

Finally, I felt his nose. I scooped the snow away from his mouth. He gasped.

I slumped forward, nearly toppling into the hole with him. Pain sliced my knee. "It's okay. I've got you," I said. "Take a breath."

Scraping farther, I uncovered the rest of his head. His face had cuts all over it. I used the shovel and the last of my energy to dig the rest of him out.

Ryan flailed to get free. I reached to guide his arms out of the backpack. He helped me pull his legs out from the hole that had entombed him.

"Are you okay?" I asked.

He crawled out on top of the snow, taking big gulping breaths. His head was bare, snow clumped in his hair. He'd lost his helmet and hat somewhere. I didn't see any injuries besides the scrapes on his face.

When I started thinking about what would've happened if I'd been a few minutes slower, my head pounded. I began to shake. We collapsed together on the snow. Melting ice cooled on my skin.

"What do we do now?" I asked my brother.

This was bad. It was too cold out here to be wet. We were miles away from the shelter. We had to get warm.

Ryan considered me for a moment as he rubbed a large bump on his head.

"Who are you?" he asked.

CHAPTER FIVE

I stared at my brother. "What?" I said.

"Who are you?" Ryan repeated, then looked around blankly. "Where am I?"

My heart broke into pieces. How could he not know me? I pulled in a shaky breath. "We were in an avalanche. I think something hit your head. I'm your twin sister. Mom and Dad don't know where we are. They think we're over on the next trail." I paused as this reality sank in. "And we have to get warm while we wait for help to come."

I glanced at our surroundings, remembering from our training that we needed to move from the base of the avalanche chute. Another avalanche could follow the same route at any minute.

Ryan picked up a handful of snow, strangely calm. "Should we make a fire?"

"Yeah, good," I said. "That's a good idea. I've got a lighter in my pack."

He was the one person in the whole world I could count on to always have my back. Even when I wanted to strangle him, I knew he was there to protect me. How could he seem so unreliable now?

Best not to dwell at the moment, I thought, on why my own brother didn't know me. I tried to rise. The pain in my knee reminded me of the thundering snow slide. I wanted to curl into a ball and wait for help. Wait for Ryan to do something. But Ryan just sat there, watching me.

We were in a deep ravine at the base of the

mountain. The wide path the avalanche took was easy to trace from the havoc of snapped trees and debris in its wake. Solid snow was packed around the trees, only the tips showing on some of them. I crawled to my pack next to the hole Ryan had been in, and reached to lift his pack too. Dragging both packs, I pulled myself toward the trees, away from the destruction the avalanche had spewed. I gritted my teeth in pain each time my knee flexed.

Ryan tried to follow me, but sank into the deep snow. He climbed back out, then looked around again. "The snow is too deep to go anywhere."

He was right. Skis would help us stay on top of the snow, but we'd both lost them. Ryan only had one pole. What were we going to do? Panic roared through my body. I focused on the packs in my hands. We had these at least.

"The skis are lost but it's okay," I said, trying to soothe us both. "We don't have to go far."

I crawled until I made it out of the danger zone and reached a tree with snow piled high on one side and a depression on the other. Ryan followed. My movements had warmed me, but Ryan was shivering. I inched over and put my hat on his bare head.

"Go collect wood for a fire," I told him, pointing into the spruce stand behind us.

He struggled to the trees and began to snap branches.

I pulled out the fire starter from my pack. Dad had just made a fire for us at lunch, so I copied everything he had done. When Ryan returned with a wide, broken tree trunk, I used that as a base for the fire so it wouldn't burn down into a hole in the snow. Then I piled dried bark and twigs on top of two fire starter sticks from my pack. When I flicked the lighter with my freezing thumb, the flames caught on the fire starter immediately, then snapped and crackled. Falling snow sizzled on the fire, but I fed it larger

twigs and the little flames grew. I made sure to zip up the lighter inside my pocket. We couldn't afford to lose it.

We held our hands toward the warmth of the fire. I glanced at Ryan's face as he sat beside me. The bump on his forehead looked worse than it had when I first pulled him out. It was swelling. Dad had the first-aid kit. Where were Mom and Dad now? Had they begun searching for us? Would they see our tracks? The falling snow seemed to answer me.

What if they didn't see our tracks?

I cupped my hands around my mouth. "HELP! We're down here!" My throat was flayed from yelling, and my voice came out hoarse. Ryan's eyes widened as he stared at me.

"They'll find us," I said, quieter. I made a snowball and lightly brushed it across Ryan's forehead. He winced. Our eyes met and my heart squeezed.

"One time when we were young, we had a fight waiting for the school bus, remember?"

Ryan blinked.

"You whipped your jacket at me so I whipped you back with mine, and the zipper hit you in the forehead. That made you even madder, so you whipped me again, harder. Both sides." I made a motion to show how he whipped the jacket at me.

"The zipper hit me on each ear. We both ran into the house crying, holding our ears and faces. Mom gave us ice cubes and told us to go catch the bus. It was coming down the hill. We hurried out and waited for the bus to stop, then climbed in, still fuming. We sat far apart from each other."

Ryan's mouth curled up a little, so I kept going.

"I had to hold an ice cube in each hand, sliding them carefully over my sore ears. The ice dripped down my forearms. When I glanced back at you, I was happy to see that you were doing the same thing to your forehead. Your face was all red and blotchy."

I looked at his face now, purple and blotchy. I smoothed back the hair that was sticking out of his hat. The snow melted and slid on his skin. "Won't be long before Mom and Dad come for us," I said.

Ryan watched me. It was eerie to see his eyes without the recognition there. He was like a different person. A more fragile Ryan.

My bottom lip quivered.

I turned to my pack and busied myself with searching for my puffy down jacket, which was compressed and sitting at the bottom. Ryan watched and pulled out his own jacket. He seemed to be doing things on autopilot.

My knee throbbed. To see it, I had to roll up my soft-shell outer pants, lightweight fleece pants, and my base layer thermals. My knee was slightly red and swollen, but didn't look as bad as it felt. I rubbed a ball of snow on it like I had done to Ryan's forehead. "I think it's sprained," I said.

"Wrap it with an elastic bandage," Ryan said.

I studied him closely. He could remember years ago when he sprained his ankle and wore an elastic bandage, but he couldn't remember *me*? Debbie Martin had pushed him off the slide at the park. He was the one who sprained his ankle, but I was the one who cried.

"That would be a good idea if we had one," I said, wishing I still had my mohair skins. But they'd been devoured, along with my skis, by the avalanche.

I dumped the contents of my pack onto my

lap and sorted through what we had. Spare fleece gloves, a spare thin hat, a frozen granola bar, and a tiny, folded emergency blanket, which was really just a thin sheet that looked like tinfoil. I stuffed the granola bar in my pocket before pulling on the gloves and hat.

There was also my transceiver, an avalanche probe, a ski repair kit with duct tape, glop stopper wax, and ski straps. No elastic bandage. My nearly empty stainless-steel water bottle was the only other thing in my pack. I filled it with snow and set it beside the fire.

Then I went through Ryan's pack. He had a multitool with a knife, his avalanche probe, a shovel, an empty water bottle, an emergency blanket, a coil of light rope, duct tape, and a candle. He filled his bottle with snow and set it next to mine. He was copying what I was doing.

All my life I had wanted to be different from my brother. To have talents that made me stand out. I don't have a smart school brain like Ryan. I'm not as athletic. Being his twin always made me even more average in comparison. And now *he* was copying *me*.

Ryan fed the fire, and the smoke drifted up and stung my eyes. The fire needed a lot of fuel to keep burning. How long would we be here? I searched the sky and noticed it was late afternoon.

I picked up the duct tape and ski straps. Could I make something for my knee? I needed something wider, stretchy. I reached into my pants and gave myself a wedgie. Using Ryan's knife, I sliced my underwear off at my hip.

Of all the days to wear my Wonder Woman undies.

I wrapped the underwear around my knee like a bandage. I flexed my knee experimentally and winced. Holding the ski straps in place with one stretched-out hand along the sides of my kneecap, I used the other to grab the duct tape. I wrapped the tape once around the top of my knee, and then again below. The tape looked like it would stay in place.

I glanced up to see Ryan watching. No joke about the underwear. Not one teasing comment from him. My throat ached. That one thing seemed to be the last straw. As I rolled my pant legs back down and tucked them into my ski boots, hot tears ran down my face.

"We're going to be okay," I said, sniffling. "They're coming to get us soon."

As I said it, the wind gusted and drove sleet into our faces. I tried not to notice the lengthening shadows. I could feel the temperature dropping already.

Even though my twin was sitting beside me, for the first time in my life I felt very alone.

CHAPTER SIX

The wind changed everything.

It sucked at the warmth from our exposed skin and open necks. Icy fingers reached into the cracks of my coat. The temperature felt like a walk-in freezer.

I raised my chin and yelled. "Hello!" My voice was brittle and cracked. "Can anyone hear us? We're alive down here!"

I listened intently for any sound of rescue. I was so sure they'd come. And now we were losing our daylight. When I glanced at my brother, seemingly helpless and confused, something snapped in me. I had to figure this out, right now. We had to get out of the wind.

"Ryan, remember when we made a quinzee at ski club?"

He shook his head. It made me angry.

"Yes, you do. I know you remember because you thought it was so cool when we piled all the snow and then hollowed it out to make a shelter. You've carried that stupid candle in your pack ever since. Remember? We all took turns sliding through the little door like a beaver house, and shared the digging. Then we had to wait for the next day to let it set. You're the one who poked the air holes. We all crammed in and lit the candles and it was warm!" My voice was getting louder and louder.

"Come on. *Remember!*" I yelled.

Ryan flinched back, his eyes blazing wild copper brown.

That settled me down instantly. "I'm sorry, it's all right. It was fun. Let's do it again, okay?

But it won't be as big, and we don't have time to let it set. We'll just dig a snow cave."

There was a hump of snow next to where the fire crackled and sparked. Using the ski pole, I rose and gingerly put pressure on my right leg. Still hurt. I took the step needed to get to the snowdrift and started digging into it with the shovel.

Ryan crawled beside me and took the shovel. For a minute, it looked like he did remember. But he just kept digging into the snow automatically.

"We have to make a ledge for the hot air," I explained. "Dig up like it's a stair step. That's it. And then dig sideways to make it like a big capital T. I'll find something to get us off the snow."

I set to work collecting spruce boughs. Parts of broken trees lay nearby, snapped off by the avalanche. Seeing them made me pause.

We could have been snapped into pieces by the avalanche.

I focused back on what needed doing and broke off some low-hanging branches from the evergreens left standing. I limped back to Ryan and piled armfuls of branches next to him before helping him dig.

My stomach pinched, telling me we had missed supper. We hadn't eaten anything since lunch and we were doing all this work out in the cold. At the club we learned about how our bodies needed fuel to keep warm in the outdoors during winter. I thought of what was in my pocket. One granola bar. Better save it for after we made the snow cave. The most important thing right now was to get shelter from the wind.

We lay on our bellies, side by side, carving into the mound to make a space big enough for both of us. Dusk was approaching fast. The light of the fire barely illuminated what we were doing.

"That's good enough. Let me try it," I said.

When I crawled in, the difference in temperature was immediate. Inside the cave the wind couldn't find me. It couldn't suck my body heat away. Being out of the cold gusts was a relief.

I looked around and shuffled in the loose, squishy snow of the floor. There was room to sit up, but not enough to stretch my legs out. The cave wasn't as good as the cozy quinzee we had made at the club. The door was much bigger, but it had to be so we could both dig at the same time in our race to beat the darkness.

I peered out at Ryan next to the fire. It had burned through the wood I'd built it on and was sinking into the snow. It needed air to breathe. The fire would die soon.

But we were not going to die soon. Not if I could help it.

CHAPTER SEVEN

I slid out of the snow cave and let Ryan drag himself in. I passed him the branches to line the floor with. The wind bit into the back of my neck. It found its way through my jacket and thoroughly chilled the sweat on my skin.

After I edged back in next to Ryan, I piled the rest of the spruce boughs behind me. The door was supposed to be just a crawl hole to keep the heat in and the cold out. I piled snow around the boughs to build a smaller opening. Then I propped up the packs in the doorway the way we did at the quinzee so we could push them out in the morning and not be sealed in by snow.

I turned to Ryan but strained to see him.

"I should have lit the candle before I closed the door," I said, fumbling in the dark. The click of the lighter was loud in the muffled stillness of our cave. Once the candle flickered shadows around the tight space, I stuck it into the ghost white wall.

"We need tinfoil like we used in the quinzee," I said. "We used it to wrap behind the candle. It helped to reflect the warmth."

I remembered our emergency blankets. Digging into the packs I found them and tore open the wrappers. When I handed Ryan his blanket, he shivered as he unfolded it and wrapped it around his body. I cut a small piece from mine to arrange with the reflective side facing the back of the candle.

"Want to make a ventilation hole?" I asked,

handing Ryan the avalanche probe. I hoped it would jog his memory.

He blankly poked a hole through the ceiling, then just as blankly passed back the probe. The loneliness of it made me bite my lip to keep from crying. I took a sip of the melted snow in my water bottle. Ryan copied with his.

Time to pull out the granola bar. "Supper's ready," I said, trying to appear to make light of our situation.

That got a spark of interest from Ryan. I carefully broke the bar in half and gave my brother the slightly bigger piece. He took it and stuffed the whole thing in his mouth.

I smiled, thinking that must be a good sign. Ryan was hungry. I chewed mine slowly, using tiny bites to make it last longer. I washed it down with more water, but it wasn't enough to fill the emptiness in my gut.

Ryan had lain down and his eyes were closed. Thinking of the long night ahead, I couldn't bear to be alone. Maybe if I reminded Ryan about things we'd done, it would bring my brother back to me.

"Last year we went to that fishing lodge on Lake Champlain," I began. "Remember, Ry?"

He looked at me. "Yeah?"

I told him about how neither one of us had wanted to touch the worms. We resorted to sticking them on the hooks, with great difficulty, while they rolled on the ground. Until Dad bent down to see what we were doing. And suddenly Ryan became brave and picked one up. He had chased me with the pulsing, slimy thing dangling from his fingers.

Through much of the cold night I told stories. I talked about the time in fifth grade when Ryan won a prize at the science fair for his universe model. Dad had been so proud when we went to the award ceremony, he told everyone we met that he was Ryan's father.

I talked about how Ryan was always winning something. How he never got into trouble at school. I was the one who did that. I reminded him how disappointed Dad had been when the school called after I got into the fight on Ryan's behalf. I had shoved Debbie Martin the next day after the sprained ankle incident. I wasn't sorry. I'd do it again.

The stories got slower as the night went on. My neck kinked, so I laid it down on my arm and tucked the emergency blanket around it. My stomach gurgled in hunger. Morning had to arrive soon. What were we going to do then?

Rescue was not coming for us. No one knew we were here. I glanced at how short the burning candle had become. We would never survive another night out here, I told myself. Not without at least a candle to cut the frost. We had to do something.

There was a snowmobile trail near where we had skied. We'd heard them roaring by when we had lunch. If we got back to the main trail, someone would come along. But we needed to get out of this ravine, back up the mountain.

How? Our skis were gone.

The problem whirled and whirled in my head. I thought of the wolverine tracks we'd seen. Of how large they were. Ryan had said the size was so they could walk on snow. We needed to make our feet big. Could we make snowshoes? I blew out a breath in frustration. I didn't know how to make snowshoes.

That was my last thought before sleep claimed me.

I jerked awake, confused by the cold blackness around me. My brain shut down. Pure terror charged through me. I was back in the hole after the avalanche! Buried alive! Wait. No, we had gotten out. I was here with Ryan. The candle had died.

"Ryan?" I groped and accidentally hit him in the face.

"Ow! What—?"

"Are you okay?" I asked, lurching up. My eyes

adjusted in the weak light filtering in from behind our packs.

"Where are we?" Ryan jerked his head around in a frenzy. "Ash?"

"Ryan," I choked out, reaching for his hand. "We're in a snow cave. You remember?"

Ryan let out a sob. He grabbed at his boots, started tearing at the buckles. "My feet! I can't feel my feet!"

CHAPTER EIGHT

"What?" I cried.

I helped Ryan unbuckle his boots. With growing panic, I noticed that his right boot was broken and split open.

Ryan ripped the boot off his foot, and my stomach rolled to see it was full of ice inside. Ryan's socks were wet. He peeled off his socks and we both stared at his waxy white feet. The baby toe on his right foot looked fake, like a mannequin's toe. The worst frostbite I'd ever seen.

Why hadn't I checked his feet instead of being so concerned with my knee? I should've had him dry out his socks! I should have at least noticed his ski boot was broken. Why didn't I take care of my brother?

"What happened?" Ryan cried. "Where are we? Where's Mom?" He struggled to rise, his legs tangling in his blanket. When he leaped up, his head crashed into the snow ceiling and he collapsed. His bare feet skidded in the tree boughs.

I took hold of him until he settled. The contact made me feel better too. Ryan was himself again. Tears of relief squeezed out of my eyes.

He panted while I told him the story. I explained to him how we built the snow cave after the avalanche. He remembered having lunch on the trail the afternoon before, but nothing later. While we talked, I pulled off my socks and helped him put them on over his cold, hard feet. The lump on his head had gone down, leaving a bluish bruise.

"I wish I had spare socks in my backpack, not just gloves," I said.

I ripped my backpack open with the knife and sliced two pieces of material from its sides to wrap my feet in before jamming them into my boots. Mine were warm and dry, but too small for Ryan's feet.

I busied myself opening the door of the cave and made sure I grabbed everything to take with us. I couldn't quite look at Ryan yet. How could I have forgotten his feet?

We had to get out of here. He needed to get his feet warm and have his head checked. Maybe the cold last night was good for his brain, but it was not good for the rest of him.

Once we were outside, Ryan pulled out the map from his pocket and we both looked up the mountain. The sky was pink and getting lighter every moment. The air felt morning chilled. Everything was quiet and still in the forest around us, as if it was on Pause.

"Do you know where the snowmobile trail is?" I asked Ryan.

He looked at the map sulkily. "Here," he said,

pointing. "Obviously. But look where we are!" He gestured around us, trying to move in the deep snow. "We'll never make it up the mountain. Without our skis we'll just sink into the snow. I can't even walk."

Ryan slumped onto his knees, still grasping the map.

"You can't give up," I said. "Come on, we can make snowshoes and walk on the snow like wolverines."

Ryan sniffed. "Mmmm..." He looked around at the trees. "Maybe if we made a frame, then use the tree boughs from the cave."

"That's it! Yes, let's figure it out. How do we make them, Ry?" A sense of gratitude washed over me at his interest. I couldn't do this alone.

Ryan pocketed the map and got up. He began to totter around in the deep snow, pulling at branches. I had thought his mind was back to normal, but now I saw he still wasn't himself—he was easily guided. My hands shook as I made another fire. I set the bottle by the fire to melt more water. We'd need to drink enough if we were going to make it out of here today. We needed food, too. I felt weak and empty.

Ryan sat beside me with two pieces of straight branches. He used the duct tape from the pack to tape the ends together. They formed a V, about as long as the distance from my waist to the top of my head. He muttered to himself as he studied what he'd made, then taped a shorter branch to join the two pieces across to form what looked like a triangle.

He bent over his project with full concentration. It made me feel calmer to see him focused. He cut two smaller branches to reach across the V in the middle like an equals sign.

"That's where your boot rests," he explained, pointing to the equals sign. "We'll fill in the empty space with tree boughs to keep us up, just like a wolverine paw, see? We'll use my rope to tie it on."

His face was determined. He looked for the moment as if he'd forgotten about his frozen

feet and where we were. I was glad. It made me afraid when he was afraid, because his emotions always photocopied to me.

We sat by the fire side by side, weaving tree boughs into the frames. Once I'd sat down, I could hear my belly. Gnawing hunger made my stomach so hollow, I felt sick. I couldn't remember ever feeling this hungry. I rubbed my belly and shivered, wishing for a big bowl of Cheerios with hot buttered toast and gobs of raspberry jam. But I needed to forget that and think about getting up the mountain. How was I going to walk with my knee injury?

"I'm starving," Ryan said.

"I don't have anything to eat," I said softly. "But when we make it up to the trail, we can eat whatever we want."

"Donuts?" Ryan asked.

"With cream inside," I said.

We tied our boots to the crosspieces so that the triangle was upside down with the pointy part behind the boot. The snowshoes looked like fuzzy slippers the way the pine needles stuck out all shaggy around my feet. I took a faltering step. Pain stabbed my knee but I tried not to let Ryan see. He shuffled behind.

I gathered our equipment and stuffed it in the one remaining backpack that I hadn't torn up. Ryan grabbed his ski pole, and we started up the mountain.

CHAPTER NINE

My boots punched through the top layer of snow, but the bushy branches I wore stopped them from sinking further. "The snowshoes are working!" I said.

They weren't easy to walk in, and they looked funny. My ski boots were also awkward, but they flexed. Slender branches of needles bounced with each step. The V of the snowshoes trailed behind me.

My feet were cold. They rubbed in the hard backpack material, but at least they weren't bare in my ski boots. Worse was my knee. It felt like it was on fire. I wondered if I should use more tape and make the brace stronger, but I didn't want to cut off the circulation. Plus there was no time to stop. I focused on putting one foot in front of the other.

"Ash," Ryan said quietly.

I turned to see his face drained of color. He pointed. That's when I saw the bear.

We watched it, a large brown hulk against the snow far above us.

"Is it looking at us?" I asked. "Did it see us? Why is it on the mountain? Aren't bears supposed to be hibernating?"

"They come out of their dens by April," Ryan said. "Is it April?"

"It will be next week," I said, disheartened that Ryan was still not okay. I needed him to be okay.

"Look," I said, pointing to the bear making its way into the distant trees with an unmistakable grizzly saunter. "It's gone now."

The bear had moved on. I hoped that was the last we'd see of it. We put our heads down and began the ascent back up toward the trail.

Ryan struggled behind me, using his pole for balance. We had no energy to speak. We needed every bit of it to keep moving upward. He let out a soft cry with each step. A large bird soared in lazy circles above us.

We could see the peak of Colt Summit clearly today without the falling snow. Jagged brown cliffs topped with heaps of pure white. My foot slipped, and I focused my gaze back onto what was in front of me. Stepping, then flicking the snow off the snowshoe with a jerk of my ankle.

Step, flick. Step, flick.

After nearly an hour of work, we were only halfway up the path the avalanche had carried us down. Ryan collapsed in a heap.

"It's no use. I can't walk," he wailed.

I'd never seen Ryan give up. It scared me more than anything. I looked around desperately. We were in the midst of the avalanche debris. Trees and rocks and chunks of ice stuck out all over the snow. My knee throbbed hotly. Ryan sat in the snow crying and shivering.

"Get up," I said. "Come on, you can do it."

I grabbed the back of his jacket and tried dragging him. I slipped and fell on my hip. Then I held on to the ski pole, balanced myself, and grabbed him again. I hauled on his dead weight as hard as I could. He didn't budge.

How were we going to make it? My legs folded and I sank into a heap next to him. I couldn't do this anymore. I wanted my parents here. I wanted Ryan to tell me it was okay, and to get up and carry me the rest of the way. I wanted to be home, wrapped in a blanket on the couch with my cat, Tiger. Have her purr on my lap and stretch her claws rhythmically.

The wind brought a cold draft down the mountain. The sky was clear blue now, sun shining. It bounced off the snow, making me squint with watery eyes. After all we'd been through, surviving an avalanche and a night in the ravine, we were going to die anyway trying to climb back up. No one would know what happened to us.

I rubbed my knee. Ryan wouldn't walk and I couldn't drag him.

I glanced up and saw the bear again. Still up the mountain, but closer. "Ryan! That grizzly is back," I whispered.

My heart pounded. It was stalking us. We were being stalked by a hungry grizzly bear that had just come out of its den. Even if I could run, there was nowhere to go. My eyes darted around. And then I saw something else.

A dark, shaggy animal was digging in the debris field behind us. Its head was broad, with short round ears. A thick yellowish stripe ran along its side from its shoulders all the way to its bushy tail. As I watched, it dug down with long claws and began to pull something out from beneath the snow.

I got Ryan's attention and gestured to the animal.

"Wolverine!" he whispered hoarsely.

We watched it fiercely tug at the back end of some dead animal with hooves and light brown hair. I couldn't tell what it was, but the carcass was bigger than the wolverine.

We were so focused on the wolverine that we didn't see the bear until it was nearly on top of us.

CHAPTER TEN

"Ryan!" I screamed.

The bear charged toward us. All I had time to do was clutch Ryan and close my eyes. Wait for the teeth.

When I heard the growl come from behind us, I twisted around to see. The bear had charged at the wolverine! Ryan and I sat where we were in the snow, holding each other. We gaped. The bear wanted the carcass, not us.

The noises coming from the wolverine made goose flesh rip up my arms. Savage growling that sounded like a Velociraptor from a dinosaur movie. A musky smell hung in the air like skunk.

The grizzly shook its head and hunched its muscled shoulders. It lunged at the wolverine but stopped short. A fake lunge. Adrenaline coursed through my body.

They circled each other warily. The bear swatted its huge paw at the ground. The paw was the size of my head. I stared at the long claws. Ryan's grip on my arm tightened as we heard the wolverine's growl grow more furious. The wolverine was clearly saying, "This is mine!"

It stood its ground in front of the bear with an attitude of a much bigger animal.

Didn't the wolverine notice the bear was twenty times its size? The wolverine did not back down. It didn't seem to consider how small it was in comparison to the enormous bear.

With a horrible growl, the wolverine flung itself onto the bear. The grizzly lurched up onto

its back legs in surprise, and then came down. It shook, then pawed at the insane devil on its neck, and the wolverine let go.

Ryan and I kept clutching each other, our shoulders leaning in. We watched the bear spin, take a few steps toward the ravine where we had just been, and then look over its shoulder. For a charged moment, no one moved. And then the bear loped away, down the mountain.

My breath puffed out in a cloud. I couldn't believe we had been able to witness this fight. We were just two specks on the middle of a mountain. Nothing out here cared whether we lived or died. Avalanches still happened, animals still hunted and fought and struggled to survive. Just like we were struggling to survive.

The wolverine turned to us then. Its shrewd gaze appraised us. I froze. *Do wolverines attack people?*

For one intense second, the wolverine and I locked eyes. We studied each other. I saw the fearlessness in its face.

I wanted to feel that way.

The wolverine turned back to the carcass and the spell was broken.

"Whoa," Ryan whispered.

"It's so beautiful," I breathed. "And wild."

The wolverine stood on its back feet with its shaggy fur hanging. It grabbed a leg of the dead animal. We kept very still and watched the wolverine tug the carcass. It made a grating sound as it slid over the snow. As we stared, the determined animal slowly dragged the entire frozen carcass into the trees behind. There was absolute silence in its wake.

Ryan and I looked at each other, not sure that what we had just seen was real.

"Did you see that?" I asked.

He nodded.

"We'll have something to tell the biologists," I said. "You wanted to get our names in the study."

I looked up the mountain with renewed determination. If a thirty-five-pound wolverine could face off with a thousand-pound bear and win, I could get us up this mountain. No matter if Ryan couldn't walk and my knee couldn't hold me. No matter how small I was in comparison to this enormous mountain. I wasn't going to quit.

But how was I going to get us there?

CHAPTER ELEVEN

I scanned the debris field, racking my brain to come up with an idea. Before the fight, I had been wishing Ryan could carry me. Peering up the mountain, I tried to imagine how I would be able to carry him.

"Climb on, Ryan," I said. I crouched next to him and offered my back. We used to give each other piggybacks all the time, though in the last few years, he'd gotten heavy. But that wasn't the biggest problem.

"In this snow?" Ryan asked. "Up a mountain? Are you sure?"

I didn't tell him about my knee. There was no other way. I had to do this. "Of course I'm sure," I said.

He wrapped his arms around me and slid onto my back. I gripped his legs, his feet dangling in the snow.

"One, two, THREE!" I strained to stand. "Agh!"

Everything in me pulled taut. My neck bulged. I stood up for a moment, wobbling. I would do this!

I took one step. My knee screamed in agony, and we both toppled forward into the snow.

We lay there gasping, sprawled on the mountain. What was I going to do? What I needed was a sled to haul my brother. I brushed at the branches of my snowshoe. Could we make a sled like we had made the snowshoes? I shook my head. I didn't know how to make a sled, even if all the materials were to drop in front of me out of a gigantic cereal box.

"It's no use," Ryan cried.

I hugged him. "Don't do that, Ry. Help me figure it out." He pushed me away.

I rolled away from him and pounded the snow in frustration. My glove hit something sharp. When I brushed the snow aside, I saw it was the side of a metal sign. Was it a caution sign from the highway? What was any kind of sign doing here in the middle of the wilderness?

I grabbed the shovel from the pack and began to dig. My arms were sore from all my digging yesterday, but I kept going. Finally, I brushed away enough snow to reveal a sign partially bolted to a torn post.

"Ryan! This is big enough for you to lie on."

He lifted his head with interest.

I wondered briefly: If the wolverine hadn't distracted us, what would've happened? If we hadn't stopped where we did, I never would have found this sign. We had the wolverine to thank.

YOU ARE ENTERING AVALANCHE COUNTRY

BEWARE OF SLOPE ANGLES MEASURING 30 AND 45 DEGREES.

BE AWARE OF SUBTLE CHANGES IN SLOPE ANGLE, ASPECT, AND ELEVATION.

AVOID WIND-LOADED SLOPES.

BEWARE OF UNUSUALLY WET OR WARM CONDITIONS AND EXTENDED PERIODS OF EXTREME COLD.

BEWARE OF ANY RAPID CHANGE IN CONDITIONS.

Colt Country Avalanche Center

ARE YOU AVY SAVVY?

"Could you hold on to the edge if I pulled you like on a toboggan?" I asked.

Ryan studied it. "You could tie what's left of my rope to the post and then loop it around your waist."

We knotted the rope tightly around the broken post at the back of the sign. Ryan rolled onto the metal sheet. He wore the backpack and clutched the top of the sign with his gloves.

"Here goes," I said. I turned to look at my brother behind me. Our eyes met.

"Are you avy savvy?" Ryan asked.

Despite everything I laughed out loud, and it felt so good. He was finally sounding more like himself. He was going to be okay.

If I could get us out of here.

I faced the mountain and leaned into the rope so I felt the weight. And then I forced myself to climb.

The pain in my knee made me gasp. Each step was torture. But the sled moved. Once the metal started sliding, I had to keep it sliding. It'd be too hard to get it going again. In order to keep up the momentum, I couldn't pause for a break. Not for one second.

My muscles screamed for me to stop. I kept

plodding with my shaggy wolverine snowshoes. One step, flick. One step, flick.

Sweat ran down my face, pooled in my shirt where the rope cut into my waist. Keep going. *Must not stop. Can't stop.* Hot stabbing pulses ripped down my leg. Had to keep going. Our lives depended on it.

I thought back to our night in the snow cave. We had no more candles. We'd surely freeze to death if we had to stay out here again. Someone had to find us on the trail.

One step.

Ryan needed to get help badly. Was he going to lose his feet? Would they turn black like I'd seen in photos of mountain climbers who had to have their feet amputated from frostbite? We had used those pictures at the club to gross each other out. Now I couldn't stop thinking about the way Ryan's feet looked.

Ryan with no feet was not how I wanted him and me to be different. Now all I wanted was for us to be the same, whole and alive.

One step.

Knives sliced through my knee. The burning reached my ankle. Must keep going. Ryan was a thousand pounds. He was a grizzly bear. I was a wolverine. I could not give up. The mountain swayed around me. I was dragging a large carcass across the snow. My feet turned into wolverine feet. Fearless feet.

One step.

I stumbled over a ridge and fell onto a hard-packed trail. My feet didn't sink. I glanced around with sudden awareness as I collapsed.

"Trail?" I croaked. "Did we make it?"

"Ash," Ryan said.

I picked up my head and tried to focus on where we were. My heart pounded in my ears. My arms quivered, barely holding up my chest.

"It's the trail!" I rasped. "Help!" I tried to scream, but only a pathetic, strangled squeak came out. I had lost my voice.

And that's when I saw the pack of wolves

running on the trail toward us. We were going to be torn to shreds after all.

Ryan raised his hand. "Help!" he yelled.

I tried getting up to run, but my legs would not work. I couldn't make them obey. Could not take one more step. I had used every ounce of will to get up the mountain and onto this trail. I covered my head with my arms.

And then they were on us. Hands reached down to grab me. *Hands?*

"Where did you guys come from?" someone said. "Hey, it must be the missing kids!"

"Are you okay?" another voice said, closer. "They've been looking for you over on Chiseler Ditch."

I looked around in confusion. I felt almost delirious with exhaustion and could hardly see straight. Was I dreaming? The wolves stood next to me in a line. Some rolled in the snow. They all had their mouths wide open, tongues hanging out.

"Sled dogs," Ryan said. He started to cry. Which made me start to cry.

We had made it. We had found the trail; it wasn't a dream. We were going to see our parents.

More people crowded around us now. They stood on the trail looking concerned and a bit startled. The dogs panted, with big smiles. Someone wrapped me in a blanket.

"You have to help my brother," I said.

CHAPTER TWELVE

Back home, two months later

"I've never heard of such tenacity," the reporter said, staring at me. He shook his head in amazement. "Most people would not have been able to persevere and keep going up that mountain."

I glanced at Dad to see him staring at me with the same expression.

"How is your knee?" the reporter asked.

I rubbed it and shrugged. "I'm still doing physical therapy for the torn meniscus. But it should be good enough to ski on next season." I knew what he was going to ask next.

"What about Ryan's feet?" he said. "Is he okay? How's his head?"

"We're still waiting for the doctors to make a decision about his baby right toe," I explained. "Whether the tissues will regenerate and heal themselves."

"Resilience" is what the doctors called it, when the body bounces back from injury. Just like his concussion. Ryan still had some memory gaps, but as long as he didn't hit his head again, his brain would be okay. He had no lasting brain injury.

"It'll be another few weeks before we know if he'll lose his toe." My throat closed up when I said it.

My brother had endured weeks of pain. His feet had swelled up. There were huge blisters, leaking pus. I'd snuck in while he was sleeping to look. But I'd kept myself busy during the day while he lay in bed. I wasn't ready to talk to him. I was afraid he was mad at me for not looking after him better. But telling the story again reminded me that I had saved Ryan's life. I had made it up the mountain and pulled him to safety with me.

Dad moved toward me and put his hand on my shoulder. "We've told you before, Ash. If he loses the toe, it's not your fault. It's because of you that he's even here. What a fighter you are." He said it like he did when Ryan won something. His eyes were shiny.

The reporter cleared his throat and turned off his recorder. "Grit is the single most important character trait for success in life." He began to pack his things.

"And my daughter's got it in spades," said Dad.

"You must be very proud of her," the reporter said.

Dad wrapped his long arms around me and pulled me in. "So proud," he said.

I let those words sink in. *Grit* and *proud*. I

may not have won any science fairs, or been the best skier on the team, but I had grit and my father was proud of me.

Ryan hobbled with his crutch through the kitchen door then. I could tell from his face that he'd been listening. Usually I sensed him near, but this time I hadn't been paying attention.

"My sister has the heart of a wolverine," he said proudly.

I raised my chin and felt something relax inside me. We looked at each other and grinned.

"And she sort of smells like one too."

I got up and jabbed him in the gut.

AUTHOR'S NOTE

As wilderness safety and technology advance, more people are venturing farther into back-country areas. Personal devices such as SPOT satellite trackers provide a feeling of greater security. Still, with more people exploring the wilderness, there is no shortage of stories of avalanche tragedies.

According to the Colorado Avalanche Information Center, over the past ten years an average of twenty-seven people died each winter in avalanches in the United States.

During my research for this book, I came across many avalanche survival stories as well. One such incident provided some inspiration, about two friends being swept up in an avalanche and one of them losing his memory as a result of head trauma. Perhaps this caught my attention because many years ago, my own brother was in a car accident and suffered a traumatic brain injury.

While this story was inspired by true events, some details are fictional, including the names of the characters and a few settings.

As always, my true interest lay in exploring the human spirit. In this story, Ashley has grit. This character trait, which gives the tenacity to persevere, is the single most important factor in survival situations. Wilderness survival begins with the right attitude. And the best example of that for me is the wolverine, the most tenacious animal and one that we have only begun to understand.

As a pivotal moment in the story demonstrates, wolverines have been known to fight off grizzlies and dig up carcasses buried under the concrete snow of avalanches. Near the Grand Teton, a study area to learn more about wolverines is part of an effort to map their behavior, range, and habitat south of the Canadian border. For more information about these extraordinary animals with large snowshoe-like paws, check out the Wolverine Foundation at www.wolverinefoundation.org.

SO, WHAT CAN YOU DO TO SURVIVE AN AVALANCHE?

AVALANCHE AND WILDERNESS SAFETY TIPS

COURTESY OF THE NATIONAL AVALANCHE CENTER, UNITED STATES FOREST SERVICE, AND THE NATIONAL PARK SERVICE

BE RESPONSIBLE: Your safety and the safety of others around you are your primary responsibilities. What you wear, where you go, the equipment you carry, and how you conduct yourself are vitally important. Find an informative introduction to the North American Avalanche Danger Scale here: youtu.be/r_-KpOu7tbA.

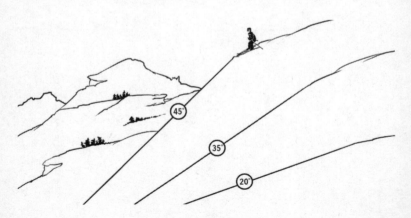

BE AVALANCHE SAVVY: Take a certified avalanche course. Know the three conditions below that must be present for an avalanche to occur.

- **Slope:** Avalanches generally occur on slopes steeper than 35 degrees.

- **Snowpack:** Recent avalanches, shooting cracks, and "whumpfing" are signs of unstable snow.

- **Trigger:** Sometimes it doesn't take much to tip the balance: people, new snow, and wind are common triggers.

THERE ARE TWO MAIN TYPES OF AVALANCHES:

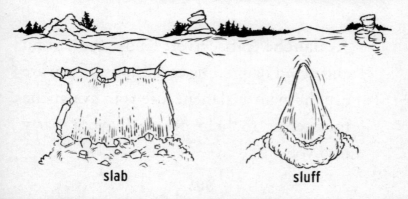

slab   sluff

- **Slab avalanches** occur when a cohesive slab of snow releases over a wide area.

- **Sluff avalanches** occur when loose superficial snow releases at a point and fans out as it descends.

BE AWARE: Know the avalanche danger and conditions where you will be recreating. Heed all warnings.

BE PREPARED: Have at least the following three safety items with you at all times and know how to use them. Everyone in your party should carry each of these items:

- **Avalanche transceiver:** Know the terrain and avoid dangerous conditions. If you are caught in an avalanche, use your avalanche transceiver to help others in your party find you.

- **Avalanche probes:** These collapsible poles are longer than ski poles and are the perfect tool to use if you need to begin searching for someone buried under the snow.

- **Shovel:** Each person in your party should carry a shovel. Shovels can help you dig others out who may be caught in an avalanche, help determine snowpack conditions, assist in leveling out an area for a tent, or be used to break down and melt snow for drinking water. Watch a video about how to use rescue tools here: youtu.be/SncL8kd8-DI.

- **Backpack:** Your pack should hold all your rescue gear, food, water, dry clothing, first-aid kit, and more. See a detailed list of items and tools to take with you when you enter backcountry here: www.fsavalanche. org/get-the-gear.

- **Partner:** None of this equipment will help you if you venture into backcountry alone. Always bring a buddy.

BE BEAR AWARE: Being outdoors means being with wildlife. Many people never encounter a bear, but if you do, you can follow some tips to keep yourself and others safe.

Bear attacks are rare; most bears are interested only in protecting their food, cubs, or space. However, being mentally prepared can help you respond effectively. The guidelines that follow provide general advice as well as different ways to respond to attacks by brown bears and black bears. Help protect yourself and others by reporting all bear incidents to a park ranger immediately. Above all, do your best to avoid an encounter. Follow viewing etiquette! Keep your distance from bears and avoid surprising them! Respect their habitat, as with all wildlife. Most bears are not interested in interfering with humans and will stay away if they hear them coming. Ask in advance about bear activity in the area where you will be hiking, and learn to recognize areas where bears are likely to be on account of a food source like berry bushes.

Remember, the most important deterrent is to keep your distance from bears! But here are some things you can do if you encounter a bear:

- Do *not* run.

- Remain calm.

- Identify yourself. If you talk calmly to the bear, the bear will recognize you as human and not a prey animal.

- Hike and travel in a group. Make yourselves look as large as possible.

- Do not allow the bear access to your food. Do not drop your pack.

- If the bear is stationary, move slowly and sideways, this allows you to keep an eye on the bear and avoid tripping. Moving sideways is also non-threatening to bears.

- Leave the area or take a detour. If this is impossible, wait until the bear moves away. Always leave the bear an escape route.

- Be especially cautious if you see a female with cubs. Never place yourself between a mother and her cub, and never attempt to approach them. The chances of an attack escalate greatly if she perceives you as a danger to her cubs.

- Carry and know how to use bear spray. It can be used to deter a charging bear.

Remember: You are responsible for your own safety and for the safety of those around you.

6.5'

5'

3'

1.5'

FIND MORE INFORMATION AT THESE WEBSITES:

www.avalanche.org

www.fsavalanche.org

www.fs.fed.us/visit/know-before-you-go

www.nps.gov/subjects/bears/safety.htm

ACKNOWLEDGMENTS

In my research for this book, I collected information from many sources, including books, reports, and transcripts. In addition, I received specialized advice from the following individuals, to whom I am grateful: Jon Stephens, game warden with the Wyoming Fish and Game Department, and Bruce Tomlinson, retired Ontario conservation officer, Ministry of Natural Resources and Forestry.

The wording on the avalanche sign that Ashley finds was inspired by the Glacier Country Avalanche Center at the Whitefish Mountain Resort.

Thank you to my critique partners, Marcia Wells and Amy Fellner Dominy, who provided feedback and encouragement.

Thanks also go to Jackie White, and to Chris and Steven White, for once again reading the manuscript and commenting like pros.

Any errors in the story are my own.

ABOUT THE AUTHOR

Terry Lynn Johnson has lived in northern Ontario, Canada, for more than forty years. She grew up at the edge of a lake, where her parents owned a lodge. For many years, she was the owner and operator of a dog-sledding business with eighteen huskies. She guided overnight trips, teaching winter survival and quinzee construction, and slept in the quinzees she helped build. During the school year, she taught dog sledding at an outdoor school near Thunder Bay, Ontario.

In addition to her personal training and experience for nearly two decades in remote areas, she has been working for the past seventeen years as a conservation officer with the Ontario Ministry of Natural Resources and Forestry. Before becoming a conservation officer, she worked for twelve years as a canoe ranger warden in Quetico Provincial Park, a large wilderness park in northwestern Ontario.

In her free time, Terry has backpacked and hiked in the mountains of Alaska, Montana, and Wyoming. She enjoys snowshoeing, skiing, and summer kayak expeditions with her husband.

Here's a sneak peek at the next book in the
SURVIVOR DIARIES series: *LOST!*

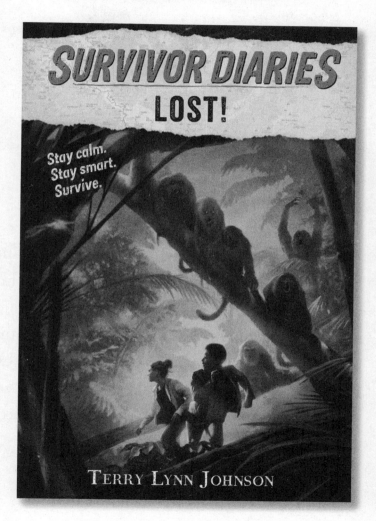

CHAPTER ONE

"Tell me, Carter. How did you survive being lost in the rainforest?" the reporter asked. He pressed Record on his phone.

I spun around on my barstool and spread my arms like the wings of a California condor. Or maybe like a trumpeter swan, with the greatest body mass of any living bird native to North America.

"Did you talk with Anna?" I asked.

"I'll be meeting with her tomorrow."

The reporter rolled up his sleeves, then produced a notepad and pen from his shirt pocket. "I want your version of what happened in Costa Rica," he continued. "This interview is for the survivor diaries I'm writing. About kids like you making it out of life-threatening situations. You're younger than Anna, only eleven years old, right?"

"Yeah—" I jumped up and turned to find the source of the squeal behind me, but it was just one of the little kids Mom babysits. I guess I still had a residue of jittery nerves.

Mom scooped up the kid. "Time for a nap, I think. I'll be right back." She headed for the stairs. I hoped she noticed I had jumped only a tiny bit.

I sat down again to face the reporter, and thought back to my time in the jungle. My hands felt clammy, and I dragged my palms across my red sweatpants. Red like the breast feathers of the resplendent quetzal. The bird that had started it all. Adding the endangered bird to my life list—all the different bird species I've seen—nearly *ended* my life.

"All right." The reporter rubbed his hairless head and looked at me expectantly. "Tell me what happened."

"The monkeys," I said. "Their calls were so terrifying. You can hear them three miles away. Did you know howler monkeys are the loudest of all the New World monkeys? That's what freaked out Anna. They were leaping overhead. The branches of the trees shook all around us. We could hear the roaring, coming closer—"

"What monkeys?" The reporter's long forehead wrinkled in confusion. "Carter, start at the beginning."

I took in a deep breath and exhaled slowly. "Okay. It all began with licking an ancient statue."

Stay calm. Stay smart. Survive.

Watch out for more books in the
SURVIVOR DIARIES series at survivordiaries.com!

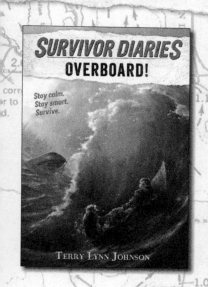

SURVIVOR DIARIES

Do you have the smarts, the grit, and the courage to survive?

— or —

Are you better off staying home?

YOU'VE READ THE BOOK, NOW PLAY THE GAME

WILL YOU SURVIVE?

survivordiaries.com